The Berenstain Bears
and the
BAD DREAM

Some dreams make cubs laugh.
Some dreams make them cry.
It's interesting to think about
what they dream and why.

A First Time Book®

The Berenstain Bears
and the
BAD DREAM

Stan & Jan Berenstain

Random House 🏠 New York

Copyright © 1988 by Berenstain Enterprises, Inc. All rights reserved.
Published in the United States by Random House Children's Books,
a division of Random House, Inc., New York.
Random House and the colophon are registered trademarks of Random House, Inc.
First Time Books and the colophon are registered trademarks of Berenstain Enterprises, Inc.
randomhouse.com/kids
BerenstainBears.com
Library of Congress Cataloging-in-Publication Data
Berenstain, Stan. The Berenstain bears and the bad dream / Stan & Jan Berenstain.
p. cm. — (A First time book)
Summary: After viewing a scary movie about the Space Grizzlies, Brother Bear has a nightmare.
ISBN 978-0-394-87341-1 (pbk.) [1. Nightmares—Fiction. 2. Dreams—Fiction. 3. Fear—Fiction.
4. Bears—Fiction.] I. Berenstain, Jan. II. Title. III. Series: Berenstain, Stan. First time books.
PZ7.B4483Bejj 1988 [E]—dc19 87-27295
Printed in the United States of America 70 69 68 67 66 65 64 63 62 61 60 59 58 57

Brother Bear was just crazy about Space Grizzlies. Space Grizzlies were little toy action figures that you could collect.

Sister Bear didn't like them much. She thought they were dumb (and a little scary).

Mama Bear didn't mind them except when Brother brought them to the table or left them on the stairs.

Papa Bear didn't care about them one way or the other.

But Brother cared about them a lot. He cared about them so much that he did chores for neighbors to make extra money so he could buy more.

DOG WALKING
10¢ PER DOG

He had quite a few. But the store had more. A lot more. He was saving up to buy Sleezo's Cloud Castle. Sleezo was the evilest of all the Space Grizzlies, and the wicked-looking Cloud Castle was where he planned all his evil deeds.

When Brother had saved enough money, he went along on a shopping trip to the Bear Country Mall and made his purchase. The Cloud Castle came in a big box, and he could hardly wait to get home to play with it. But as he was getting into the car, he saw something that was even more exciting than the Cloud Castle.

It was a movie poster. It said:
COMING SOON. SPACE GRIZZLIES—
THE MOVIE!

"A Space Grizzlies movie!" he cried. "It looks great! I can't wait to see it!"

"I can," said Sister. "Looks scary to me."

"May I see it when it comes, Mama?" asked Brother. "May I? May I, please?"

"Hmm," said Mama. "We'll see when the time comes."

When they got home, Brother opened his new Cloud Castle, got out all his Space Grizzlies, and was all set to play the biggest Space Grizzly game ever. *But*...he had nobody to play with. Nobody, that is, except Sister.

"Want to play Space
Grizzlies, Sis?" he asked.
"No way," she said.
"Aw, come on," he said. "I'll
play any game you want if you'll
play Space Grizzlies with me."

"Any *three* games," she said,
driving a hard bargain.
"Which three?" he asked warily.
"Paper dolls, jacks, and beanbags,"
she answered.
"Paper dolls, jacks, and beanbags!"
he protested. "Give me a break!"
"Take it or leave it," she said.

He took it. And after some lively sessions of paper dolls, jacks, and beanbags, it was time for...

—SPACE GRIZZLIES!

"I am Sleezo, evil king of the universe!" roared Brother. "Calling all spaceships! Seek and destroy the planet Magongo, home of my sworn enemy, Heero the Magnificent!"

"Oh, no, you don't!" Sister shouted back. "I am Heero the Magnificent! One touch from my sleep wand and your evil ways will be ended!"

They played until Mama called them for dinner.

"Brother," said Mama, "how many times must I tell you—no Space Grizzlies at the table!"

Papa was taking a peek at the *Bear Country News*. "Brother," he said, "that movie of yours starts tomorrow."

"May I see it, Mama, please?" asked Brother.

"I don't know why not," she said. "We haven't been to the movies in a while."

"I know why not," said Sister.
"Because it's scary."
"That's no problem," said Papa.
"There are lots of movies
to choose from."

He was right. The Bear Country
Theater was really four movie houses
in one, and there were usually four
different movies playing.
"This looks good," said
Mama. *The Magic
Toeshoes*. It's a musical
about a ballerina."

So when they got to the movies the next evening, Mama, Papa, and Sister got in line for *The Magic Toeshoes*, and Brother joined a bunch of his friends in line for *Space Grizzlies*.

The Magic Toeshoes told the story of a young bear who wanted to be a ballerina. But every time she tried to dance on her toes she wiggled and wobbled. The old ballet master took pity on her and gave her a pair of magic toeshoes which cured her wiggles and wobbles.

But on the night of the big ballet, she left her magic toeshoes on the bus! Without them she was all wiggles and wobbles again. That's when the ballet master told her they weren't magic at all! They were just ordinary toeshoes. The wobbly ballerina got her confidence back and danced beautifully ever after.

The Space Grizzly movie was about Space Grizzlies, of course: great monstrous big-screen ones who zapped and zoomed through space until that final intergalactic shootout. It was very exciting and *not a little scary.*

It was dark when the Bear fami
got home, so it was off to bed
for the cubs. It was already late
for Sister, and she went right
to sleep. But Brother was so
excited by the movie that he lay
awake for quite a while. He was
just about to doze off when
Sister woke up screaming.

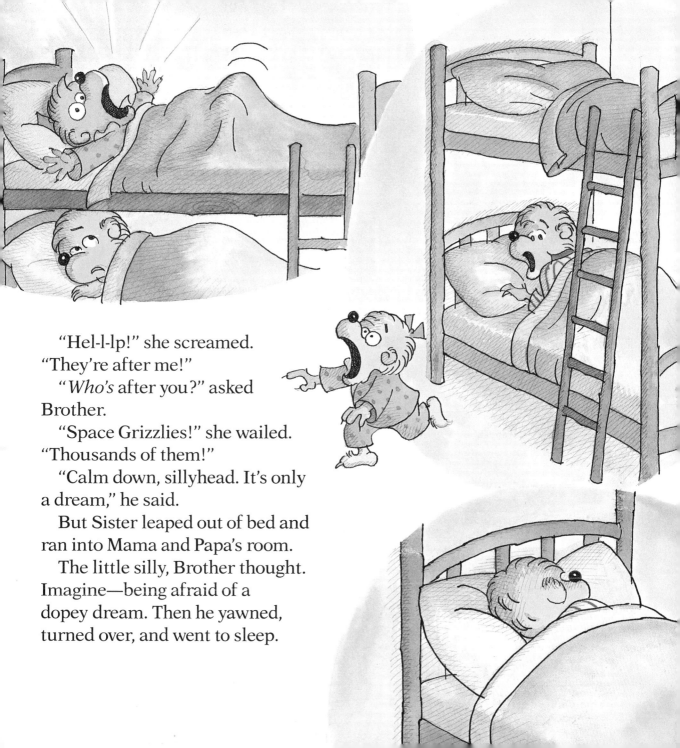

"Hel-l-lp!" she screamed. "They're after me!"

"*Who's* after you?" asked Brother.

"Space Grizzlies!" she wailed. "Thousands of them!"

"Calm down, sillyhead. It's only a dream," he said.

But Sister leaped out of bed and ran into Mama and Papa's room.

The little silly, Brother thought. Imagine—being afraid of a dopey dream. Then he yawned, turned over, and went to sleep.

Mama and Papa tried to calm Sister. They took her into their bed and hugged her.

"Tell us about your dream," said Mama.

"Dream?" Sister said.

"Yes," said Papa. "You must have had a nightmare. That's the word for a bad dream."

"But it was so *real*!" she said, calming down a bit.

"That's how it is with dreams," he said. "It's as if they're really happening, but they're not—they're just in your mind."

"Can you tell us your dream?" asked Mama.

"It was awful!" Sister said. "I was a ballet star dancing on my toes, and then the stage turned into a giant beanbag board and the Space Grizzlies came out of the beanbag holes and chased me and I fell down one of the holes.

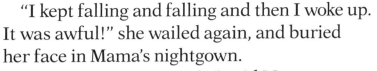

"I kept falling and falling and then I woke up. It was awful!" she wailed again, and buried her face in Mama's nightgown.

"I'm sure it was, sweetie," said Mama. "But it was also very interesting."

"Interesting?" Sister said in a puzzled voice.

"Oh yes," said Mama. "You see, even though you go to sleep, your mind keeps right on thinking. But it doesn't think in a sensible way. It takes all the things you were thinking or were nervous about during the day and puts them together all jumbled like a mixed-up jigsaw puzzle."

"You mean—like the ballet dancer from the movie?" said Sister.

"Sure," said Papa.

"And the beanbag board from playing beanbags with Brother—" she added.

"And the Space Grizzlies—" began Mama.

"Were from playing Space Grizzlies with Brother and from seeing the movie poster!" Sister said.

"Exactly," said Papa.

"Say," she said. "That *is* interesting!"

That's when they heard Brother.

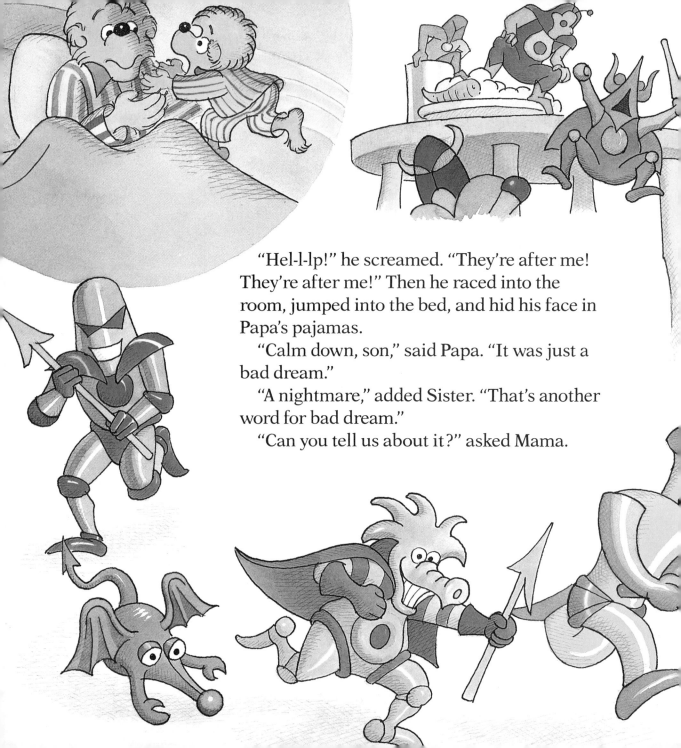

"Hel-l-lp!" he screamed. "They're after me!
They're after me!" Then he raced into the
room, jumped into the bed, and hid his face in
Papa's pajamas.

"Calm down, son," said Papa. "It was just a
bad dream."

"A nightmare," added Sister. "That's another
word for bad dream."

"Can you tell us about it?" asked Mama.

"Well, I was eating dinner and the food turned into Space Grizzlies—gigantic ones, and they chased me and I turned into a paper doll and my clothes were flying off! It was awful!"

"You're awake now, dear," said Mama. "Everything's going to be all right."

"But Mama," he said, "it was so real."

"Of course it was," said Sister. "That's the way dreams are. Let me explain it to you."

And she did.